**W9-BYA-812**

# Dear Parents:

Congratulations! Your child is taking the first steps on an exciting journey. The destination? Independent reading!

**STEP INTO READING®** will help your child get there. The program offers five steps to reading success. Each step includes fun stories and colorful art or photographs. In addition to original fiction and books with favorite characters, there are Step into Reading Non-Fiction Readers, Phonics Readers and Boxed Sets, Sticker Readers, and Comic Readers—a complete literacy program with something to interest every child.

## Learning to Read, Step by Step!

### Ready to Read  Preschool–Kindergarten
• **big type and easy words** • **rhyme and rhythm** • **picture clues**
For children who know the alphabet and are eager to begin reading.

### Reading with Help  Preschool–Grade 1
• **basic vocabulary** • **short sentences** • **simple stories**
For children who recognize familiar words and sound out new words with help.

### Reading on Your Own   Grades 1–3
• **engaging characters** • **easy-to-follow plots** • **popular topics**
For children who are ready to read on their own.

### Reading Paragraphs  Grades 2–3
• **challenging vocabulary** • **short paragraphs** • **exciting stories**
For newly independent readers who read simple sentences with confidence.

### Ready for Chapters  Grades 2–4
• **chapters** • **longer paragraphs** • **full-color art**
For children who want to take the plunge into chapter books but still like colorful pictures.

**STEP INTO READING®** is designed to give every child a successful reading experience. The grade levels are only guides; children will progress through the steps at their own speed, developing confidence in their reading. The F&P Text Level on the back cover serves as another tool to help you choose the right book for your child.

Remember, a lifetime love of reading starts with a single step!

# To
# Gabriel Giattino

All rights reserved. Published in the United States by Random House Children's Books, a division of Penguin Random House LLC, New York.

Step into Reading, Random House, and the Random House colophon are registered trademarks of Penguin Random House LLC.

Visit us on the Web!
StepIntoReading.com
randomhousekids.com

Educators and librarians, for a variety of teaching tools, visit us at
RHTeachersLibrarians.com

*Library of Congress Cataloging-in-Publication Data*
Names: Hayes, Geoffrey, author, illustrator.
Title: The mystery of the riverboat robber / by Geoffrey Hayes.
Description: New York : Random House, [2016] | Series: Step into reading. Step 3 |
Summary: Otto the alligator wants to be a hero like Uncle Tooth, so he follows the shady figure who is skulking around the riverboat docked in the harbor.
Identifiers: LCCN 2015038770 | ISBN 978-0-553-52053-8 (pbk.) | ISBN 978-0-375-97470-0 (lib. bdg.) | ISBN 978-0-553-52054-5 (ebook)
Subjects: | CYAC: River boats—Fiction. | Alligators—Fiction. | Animals—Fiction. | Mystery and detective stories. | BISAC: JUVENILE FICTION / Mysteries & Detective Stories. | JUVENILE FICTION / Action & Adventure / General.
Classification: LCC PZ7.H31455 Myh 2016 | DDC [E]—dc23

Printed in the United States of America
10 9 8 7 6 5 4 3 2 1

This book has been officially leveled by using the F&P Text Level Gradient™ Leveling System.

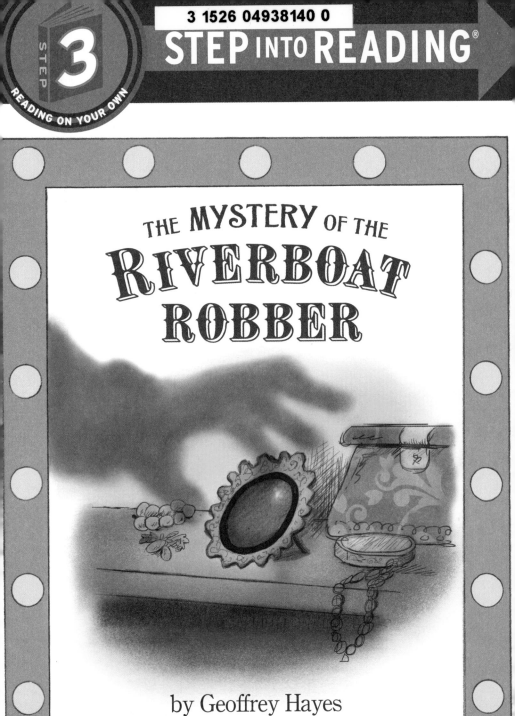

# THE MYSTERY OF THE RIVERBOAT ROBBER

by Geoffrey Hayes

Random House New York

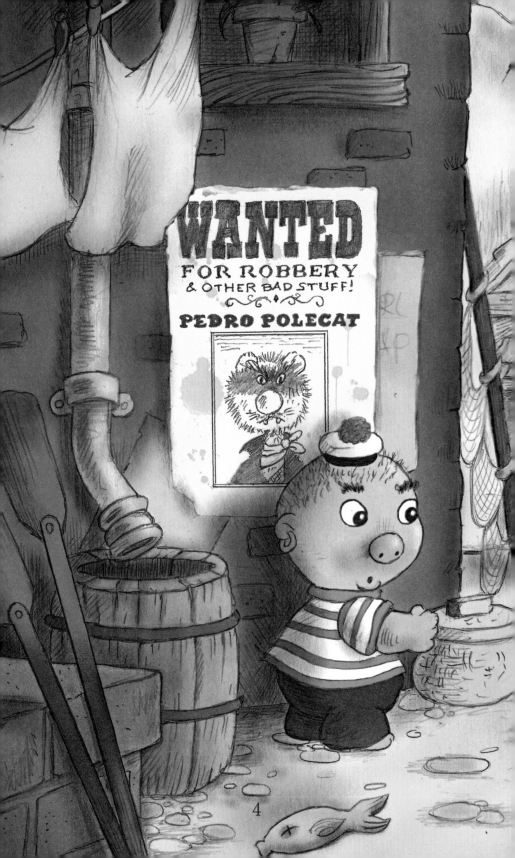

4

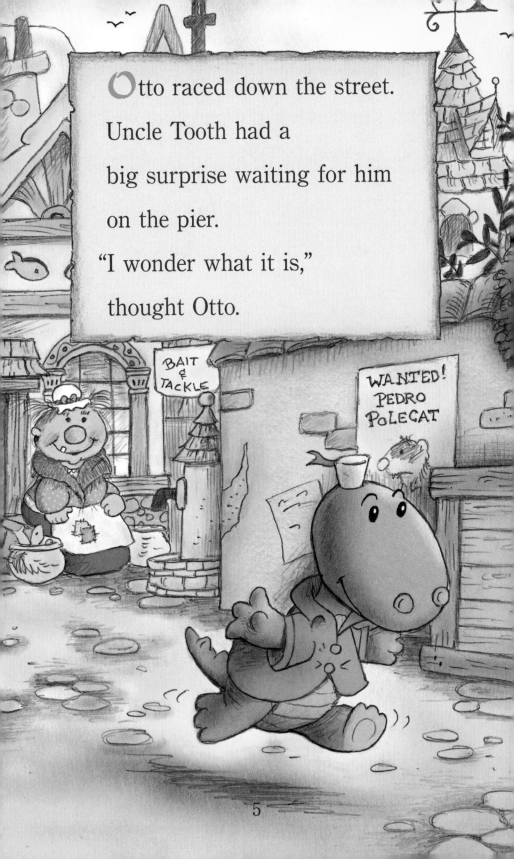

Otto raced down the street.
Uncle Tooth had a
big surprise waiting for him
on the pier.
"I wonder what it is,"
thought Otto.

BAIT & TACKLE

WANTED!
PEDRO
POLECAT

As soon as he reached the pier,
he knew what the surprise was.
A big boat with a paddle wheel
and two smokestacks
was docked at the harbor—
a riverboat!

Uncle Tooth was on deck
with a lady alligator.
"Say hello to my old friend
Lizzie Mae Falloon.
She is a famous actress.
We have tickets
for her show tonight."

"Pleased to meet you," said Otto.

"I'm training to be a hero

like Uncle Tooth."

Lizzie Mae unclipped
something from her dress
and handed it to Otto.
"In that case, you can guard
my lucky pin for me.
I never go onstage without it."

"We're going for a walk
to share old memories,"
said Uncle Tooth.
"Why don't you stay
and explore the riverboat
until we get back?"
"Sure thing!" said Otto.

The riverboat
had three decks.

It had a kitchen
and a stage.

It even had dressing rooms.

Otto heard a noise.

He poked his head

around Lizzie Mae's door.

A tall fellow was hunting
through Lizzie Mae's wardrobe.

"What are you doing?"

Otto asked.

The tall fellow spun around.

He had a fine set of teeth.

"I am Edgar La Ruse.

I play the part of Slippery Slim.

I was just hired yesterday.

I thought this was

*my* dressing room."

As he was leaving,
Edgar La Ruse saw the pin
in Otto's hand.
"That's Lizzie Mae's pin.
Did you steal it?" he asked.
"No," said Otto.
"Lizzie Mae told me
to guard it."
Otto did not trust
Edgar La Ruse.

Otto looked around some more.

Then he went on deck.

He saw a lady crying.

"Something wrong, miss?"

"Hello," the lady said.

"I am Lizzie Mae's sister,

Lizzie Lou.

I promised to clean her lucky pin,

but I forgot where she keeps it."

"I have it!" cried Otto.

"Lizzie Mae told me to guard it."

The lady stopped crying and said,

"It seems she forgot to tell you.

She wanted it to sparkle

in the show tonight."

"Well, I guess it's okay," said Otto.

"Since you *are* her sister."

Lizzie Lou grabbed the pin.

As she hurried off,

Otto saw a polecat tail

sticking out of her dress!

"That's not Lizzie Mae's sister.

That's Pedro Polecat!" cried Otto.

"I'll bet he is also Edgar La Ruse!"

Pedro leapt over the railing.

He landed on the paddle wheel.

The pin went flying!

Otto caught it!
He ran to
the rear of the boat
and slipped through
a porthole.

Otto found himself backstage.
There were props.
There was scenery
and lots of rope.

Otto heard footsteps.

He hid in an old trunk

until the footsteps passed.

"I have to get off this boat

without Pedro catching me,"

thought Otto.

Inside the trunk were costumes.

He put one on.

Otto went onstage.

The way to the door was clear.

Or was it?

Otto made his voice high.

"Help, mister.

There is a mean little alligator

backstage with a pin.

He pushed me down!"

Pedro pulled off Otto's wig.

"Really? I thought he was right here,"
said Pedro.

Otto ran back to the stage.

Pedro followed him.

"Where are you?" Pedro growled.

"I'm right here," cried Otto.

He pulled on some rigging.

The rope caught Pedro's foot,
and he was snared.
"Looking for this?" said Otto.

Pedro laughed.

Otto looked at the pin.

It was bent

and the jewel was missing!

"Oh, no!" cried Otto.

"I must have sat on it

when I hid in the trunk!"

Otto heard Uncle Tooth
and Lizzie Mae calling him.
"Here I am," said Otto.
"What is going on?"
asked Uncle Tooth.
"Edgar La Ruse is Pedro Polecat.
He was trying to steal
Lizzie Mae's lucky pin!"

Lizzie Mae tore off
Pedro's fake mustache.
"I thought there was
something phony about you,"
she said.

Lizzie Mae hugged Otto.

"You are my hero," she said.

"No, I'm not," Otto replied.

"I broke your pin.

Now you can't wear it

in the show tonight."

Lizzie Mae laughed.

"I was playing

a little game with you.

That is just a fake.

I keep my *real* pin

in my safe."

What a relief!

The police came

and led Pedro away.

Lizzie Mae sighed.

"Now that Pedro is gone,

who will play the role of

Slippery Slim in tonight's show?"

"I can do it!" cried Otto.

"Why, Otto," said Lizzie Mae,

"you truly *are* a hero!"

The show was a big hit.

Lizzie Mae wore her lucky pin.

The actors got a standing ovation.

It was so loud that
Pedro could even hear it
from his prison cell.